GiRL POWER

5-MiNUTE STORIES

1o Books in 1

HOUGHTON MiFFLiN HARCOURT
BOSTON NEW YORK

CONTENTS

I Like Myself!

by Karen Beaumont
Illustrated by David Catrow

Wishing every child the magic of self-acceptance and love —K.B.

To Jeanette, for pushing me outside the envelope —D.C.

I like myself!

I'm glad I'm me.

There's no one else
I'd rather be.

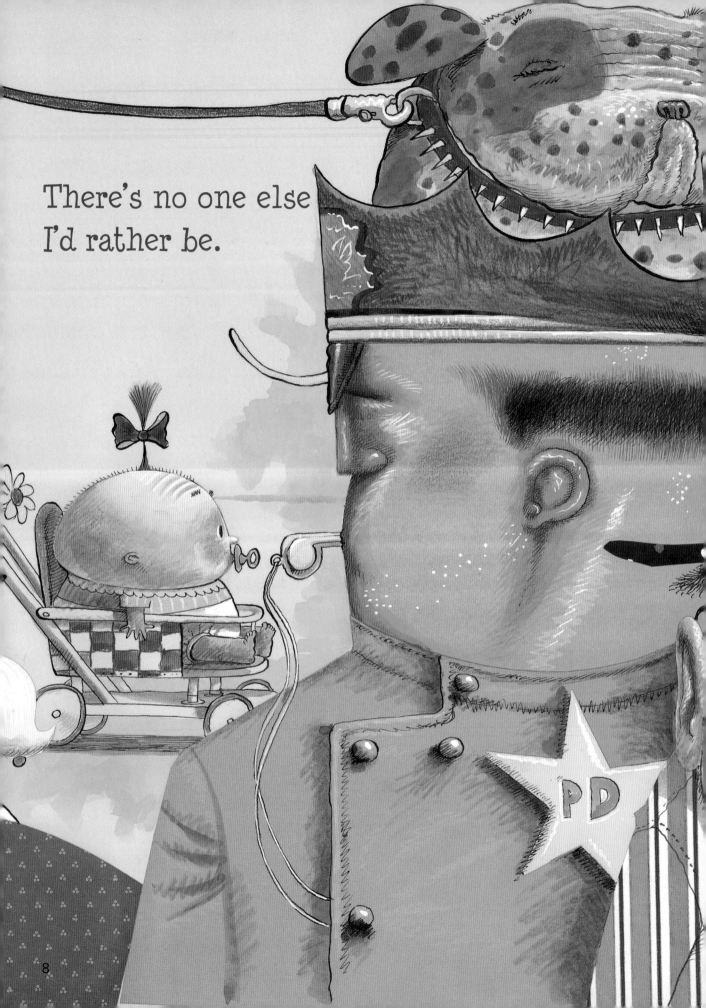

I like my eyes, my ears, my nose.
I like my fingers and my toes.

I like me wild.
I like me tame.
I like me different
and the same.

I like me fast.
I like me slow.
I like me
everywhere I go.

I like me on the inside, too,
for all I think and say and do.

Inside, outside, upside down,
from head to toe and all around,
I like it all! It all is me!
And me is all I want to be.

And I don't care
in any way
what someone else
may think or say.

18

I may be called a silly nut
or crazy cuckoo bird—so what?
I'm having too much fun, you see,
for anything to bother me!

Even when I look a mess,
I still don't like me any less,
'cause nothing in this world, you know,
can change what's deep inside, and so . . .

No matter if they stop and stare,
no person—ever—anywhere
can make me feel that what they see
is all there really is to me.

I'd *still* like me with fleas or warts,
or with a silly snout that snorts,

or knobby knees or hippo hips
or purple polka-dotted lips,

or beaver breath or stinky toes
or horns protruding from my nose,

or—yikes!—with spikes all down my spine,
or hair that's like a porcupine.

I *still* would be the same, you see . . .

I like myself because I'm **ME!**

SUPERSISTER

by BETH CADENA

Illustrated by FRANK W. DORMER

For Lynn and Kate and Joe —B.C.

To Mike/Meegs/Mono/Uncle Claw—the best SuperBrother I know —F.W.D.

Supersister bounds out of bed. Another super day.

Hark! A call from the kitchen. Mother is in need.

Supersister dashes down the stairs like a whistling locomotive.

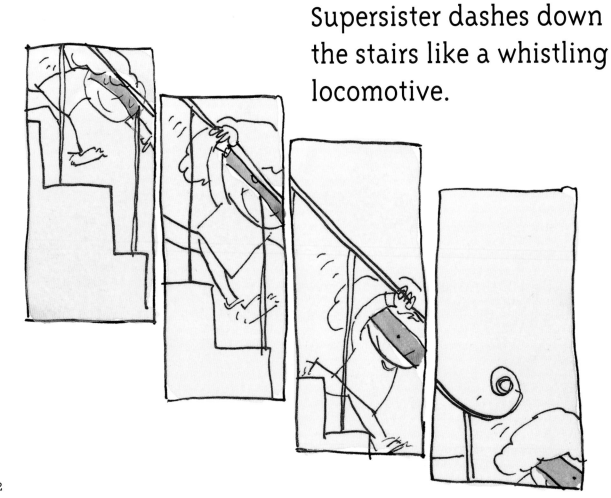

She rescues the cereal box from Mother's weary hand. This is a job for Supersister.

She pours!

She spoons!

She spills—

a little.

It's time for school. Backpacked and buttoned, Supersister is determined to strike out for the bus stop alone.

She looks back only twice.

(Even Supersister likes to know Mother is watching.)

Wait! Supersister has forgotten two things.

She races home for a kiss and to tie Mother's shoes.

At school, Supersister dots all of her i's. She crosses all of her t's. She thinks up three new ways to help Mother.

After school, Supersister springs into action.
First, she takes her dog, Poopsie, for a walk.
Supersister is a super dog walker.

She runs! She skips! She scoops!

She doesn't step in anything. Almost.

Next, she sets the table for dinner.

Supersister is a super setter. Plates. Cups. Forks.

She doesn't
drop a thing.

YES!

After dinner, she reads a story to Poopsie.

Supersister is a super reader.

She reads the story thirteen times. Super loud.

Supersister has been a super helper. She'll think up more ways to help Mother tomorrow.

Now it's time for bed.

Of course Supersister tucks herself in.

She calls out only six times.

Make that seven.

(Even Supersister likes to know Mother is listening.)

Supersister counts sheep to fall asleep.
One sheep, two sheep . . . ten sheep. Wait!

Supersister has forgotten two things.

She hurries downstairs for a kiss and to
untie Mother's shoes.

She pats Mother's enormous belly.
"Like I always say, you're going to be a
super sister," says Mother.

"Soon?" asks Supersister.
"Very soon," says Mother.

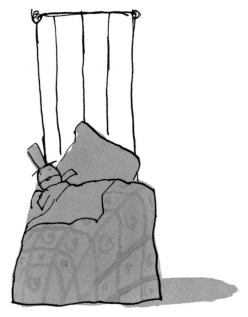

Supersister bounces
back to bed.

She counts just one woolly sheep.

She dreams her super sister dream.

Another super night.

Tallulah's Tutu

by MARILYN SINGER

Illustrations by

ALEXANDRA BOIGER

To the ballet students at the Third Street Music School Settlement
—M.S.

To Xenia and Sal, with love
—A.B.

TALLULAH just knew she could be a great ballerina—
if only she had a tutu.

"And maybe a lesson or two," her mother said with a wink.

53

So the next day, Tallulah went to her very first ballet class.
The kids wore leotards and pink tights. All except one.

He had on black pants. **A boy in ballet? Well, HE won't get a tutu.** Tallulah giggled.

"Are you with us, Tallulah?"
asked her teacher.

Tallulah decided she'd
better pay attention.
She turned out her feet and
curved her hands near her hips
in first position. She bent her
knees in a plié.

**I am an excellent
ballerina,** she thought.
And soon, I'll get a tutu.

At the end of class, the teacher
told them what a good job they'd done.
Tallulah waited for her tutu.

But instead she got a hug.
"Good job," her teacher said.

Tallulah decided that
her tutu must be coming
from Paris. They would
fly it in next week.

Tallulah practiced every day.
"Look at my beautiful arms," she
said on the way to class. "Look at
my perfect finish!"

She grinned a big grin as she stood at the barre. "What color tutu do you want?" she asked the girl in front of her. "I want lavender!" She pointed to some September asters blooming outside the window.

"Tallulah, look in the mirror. Can you make your back straighter?" her teacher said.

Tallulah could. She jumped her heels apart to second position. She pointed her toe in a tendu. She circled her foot on the floor in a rond de jambe.

I am a fabulous ballerina, Tallulah told herself. **I'm going to get my tutu right after class.**

But this time all she got was a kiss on the top of her head. "Keep it up, Tallulah. You're doing well," said her teacher.

Tallulah figured the delivery truck broke down. Her tutu must be stuck in New Jersey. They would drive it in next week.

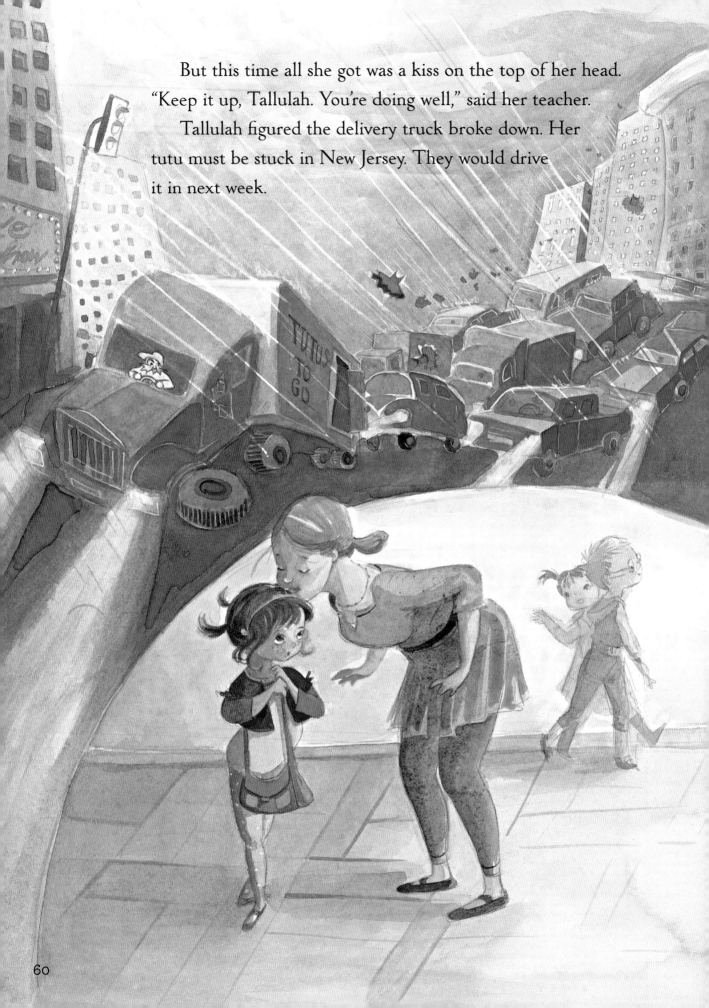

At her third lesson, she could hardly keep still. "One-two-three. One-two-three," she sang to the boy next to her. "A tunic for you, a tutu for me." She whirled around and bumped his leg.

"Tallulah, stay in your own space, please," her teacher said.

"Whoops," Tallulah said.

She shifted one foot in front of the other in third position.

She put one foot against her other knee in a passé.

She did a relevé by standing on her toes.

I'm the best ballerina in the world,
Tallulah said to herself.
Today I'll get my tutu for sure!

But there was no tutu for Tallulah. No tutu at all.

"Where is it?" she asked her teacher.

"Where is what?"

"My tutu."

Tallulah's teacher leaned down. "You have to wait awhile, Tallulah.
It takes time and a lot of practice to earn your tutu."

Tallulah stamped her foot. It did not feel good to do that in a ballet slipper.
"That's not fair!" she cried. "A ballerina needs a tutu, and she needs it now!"

Tallulah decided she wasn't going to practice any more ballet. She told her mother that she wasn't going to show her any more steps. And she wasn't going to go to class ever again.

"Really?" said her mother. "But I thought you loved ballet."

"*I* love ballet," said Beckett, her little brother, even though he'd never taken a class.

"Well, *I don't.* I'm not even going to *think* about ballet anymore," Talullah declared.

But everything kept reminding Tallulah of ballet.
And everywhere she went, Tallulah couldn't help *dancing* ballet.

She always did a plié when she patted
the neighbor's dog,

and she couldn't go by a store window
without doing a beautiful finish

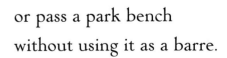

or pass a park bench
without using it as a barre.

Then, one day in the supermarket, she heard tinkly music over the loudspeakers. It was the same music the pianist played in her class. Tallulah couldn't stop herself.

Passés,
relevés,
        tendus... she did them all!
She pirouetted around the store.

When she finished, the shoppers applauded. Except for one girl.
She was wearing a lavender tutu. "I want to dance like that," she said.
"I've already got the tutu."

"Maybe you need a lesson or two. Or *twenty*-two," Tallulah said.
"And lots of practice as well." She looked at her mother and winked.

The next day she went back to class. "I'm glad to see you, Tallulah," said her teacher.

Tallulah beamed. "I'm glad to see you, too," she said. Then she took her place at the barre.

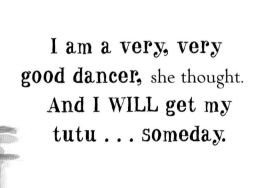

I am a very, very good dancer, she thought. And I WILL get my tutu . . . someday.

And she did. Except it wasn't lavender.
It was as red as the roses blooming that June.

Flora's Very Windy Day

by JEANNE BIRDSALL

illustrated by MATT PHELAN

For Kelsey and Jesse —J.B.

For all the big sisters I know —M.P.

"Mommy! Crispin spilled my paints again!" shrieked Flora.

"I told you to keep your paints out of his reach," said her mother.

"I tried," said Flora, "but—"

"Oh, look at this mess. Outside, Flora. Right now!"

"I can't go outside," protested Flora. "The wind is very strong and will blow me away."

"Nonsense," said her mother.

Flora thought for a moment. "Of course, I could wear my super-special heavy-duty red boots. They'll keep me from being blown away."

"Fine," said her mother. "And take Crispin with you."

Now, Crispin did not have super-special heavy-duty red boots to protect him from the wind. His boots were purple and couldn't do anything but keep his feet dry.

Oh, well, Flora thought. It wouldn't be *her* fault if Crispin blew away.

So Flora put on her coat and hat and her super-special heavy-duty red boots.

And her mother put Crispin into his little coat and hat and regular old purple boots.

And when all that was done, Flora's mother opened the door and Flora and Crispin stepped outside.

The wind was indeed very strong that day. It pushed and pulled, and twirled and twisted. But no matter how hard it blew, Flora stayed firmly on the ground.

"Ha ha! You dumb wind," said Flora. "You can't lift me up, because I'm wearing my super-special heavy-duty red boots!"

The wind did not like being laughed at. It doubled its strength and blasted mightily at Flora, but still she didn't budge.

"However," said Flora, "you may notice that my little brother is wearing regular old purple boots."

Now the wind tripled its strength. It swirled and swooped, and whizzed and walloped, and then—oh, my!—Crispin was being lifted off the ground.

Just a little bit at first, but the wind grew stronger and Crispin went higher, and then higher, and then higher still.

He was being blown away.

He looked very frightened.

And suddenly Flora was kicking off her super-special heavy-duty red boots and spreading her coat to the wind and—oh, my, oh, my!—she was sailing up toward Crispin.

She grabbed his hand and
closed her eyes and wished she
were anywhere else in the world.

But soon Flora realized that being blown by the wind was comfortable, like riding along on a squishy flying chair. She decided to open her eyes.

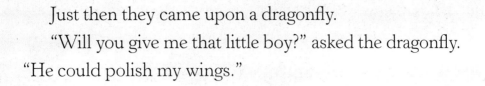

Just then they came upon a dragonfly.

"Will you give me that little boy?" asked the dragonfly.

"He could polish my wings."

"Silly dragonfly," scolded Flora. She knew that Crispin was too clumsy to clean such delicate wings. "He's my brother and I'm taking him home."

"If the wind lets you," said the dragonfly.

Flora and Crispin flew on and on until they came
upon a rainbow.

"Will you give me that little boy?" asked the
rainbow. "He could guard my pot of gold."

"Gold!" That was tempting. But, thought Flora,
Crispin's not fierce enough to guard anything. "No.
He's my brother and I'm taking him home."

"If the wind lets you," said the rainbow.

Flora and Crispin flew on and on
until they came upon a cloud.
"Will you give me that little boy?"
asked the cloud. "He could squeeze
out my raindrops."

Flora thought that squeezing out raindrops sounded like fun.
But Crispin would surely catch a cold, and then who would help
him with his nose? "No, I won't give him to you. He's my brother
and I'm taking him home."

"If the wind lets you," said the cloud.

Flora and Crispin flew on and on until they came upon the
man in the moon.

"Will you give me that little boy?" asked the man in the moon.
"It's lonely up here, and he could keep me company."

The man in the moon had a kind face, and he did look awfully
lonely. But there were no chocolate chip cookies on the moon, and
Crispin was so fond of chocolate chip cookies. "I'm sorry, but I
can't," said Flora. "He's my brother and I'm taking him home."

"If the wind lets you," said the man in the moon.

Flora stomped her foot—or would have if there'd been anything to stomp on. "I'm tired of hearing that. Why won't the wind let us go home?"

"You should ask him," answered the man in the moon.

Flora hadn't thought of that. "Oh, wind, will you let us go home?"

"I'll let *you* go home as soon as we find the right spot for Crispin," replied the wind. "You do want to get rid of him, right?"

"Yes. I mean, I did. I mean—" Flora wasn't sure what she meant.

"Because I could even use him myself," said the wind. "You know, to work my bellows."

"No, thank you." Flora had finally
decided. "I should take him home.
My mother wouldn't like it if
I lost him."

"If that's what you really want,"
said the wind.

"Yes, please," said Flora.

So the wind turned Flora and Crispin
around and blew them home.

Flora put her super-special heavy-duty red boots
back on, then straightened Crispin's hat and brushed
a shred of rainbow from his coat.

She rang the doorbell and her mother opened the door.

"I decided to bring Crispin back," Flora told her.

"From where?" asked her mother.

"From the moon," said Flora.

"Nonsense," said her mother. "Now come inside. I've made chocolate chip cookies."

PRINCESS IN TRAINING

Tammi Sauer

Pictures by
Joe Berger

For the royally awesome Julia, Madison, Sierra, and Adalie —T.S.

For princesses Matilda, Beatrice, and Martha —J.B.

Viola Louise Hassenfeffer
was not an ordinary princess.

The kingdom was beside itself.
"She's supposed to be prim,"
said the king.
"She's supposed to be proper,"
said the queen.

Then one day Viola
received a letter.

Dear Viola Louise Hassenfeffer:

Do you want to polish your princess skills?
Camp Princess will teach you to wave,
walk, and waltz just like royalty should.
The day concludes with the Royal Bash.

Enroll now so you can be the darling
of your kingdom!

Sincerely,
Director of Camp Princess

Madame Gertrude

Viola grinned.
Me? The darling
of the kingdom?

She whooshed
off to give Camp
Princess a try.

"Welcome to Camp Princess, ladies,"
said Madame Gertrude.

"Let's begin with the Royal Wave."

The princesses worked on good posture,
practiced proper elbow placement, and
added the customary turn of the wrist.
Princess Viola's wave was nice, but she
thought it could use a little OOMPH.

HI-YAH!

"Viola Louise Hassenfeffer!" called her teacher. "Royalty does not karate-chop."

"Oops." Viola ducked behind a sea of up-dos.

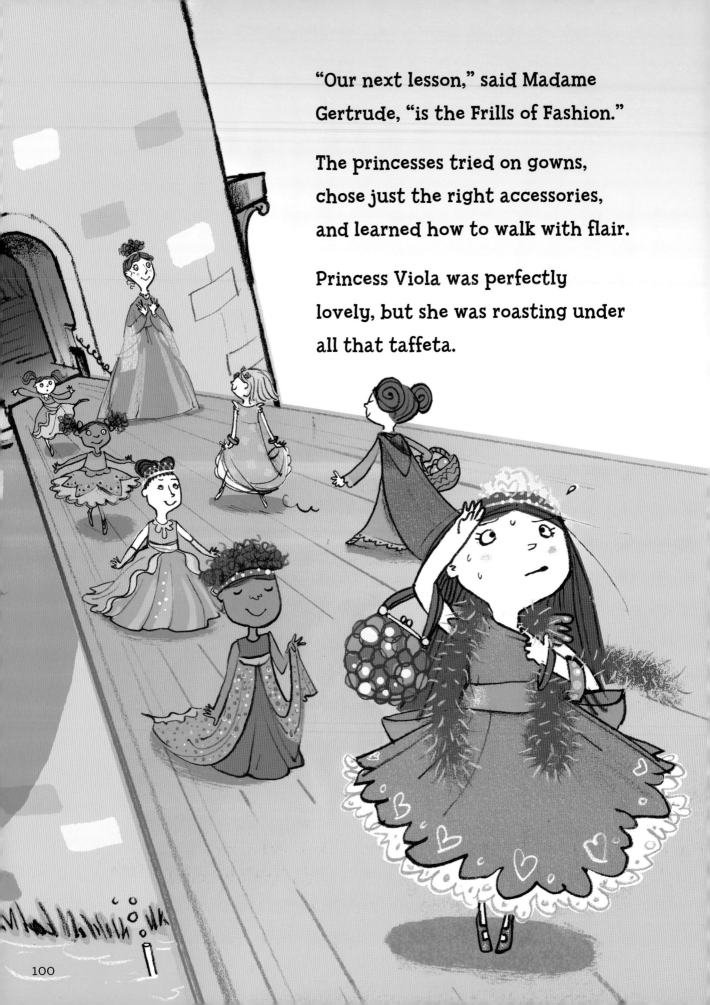

"Our next lesson," said Madame Gertrude, "is the Frills of Fashion."

The princesses tried on gowns, chose just the right accessories, and learned how to walk with flair.

Princess Viola was perfectly lovely, but she was roasting under all that taffeta.

SPLASH!

"Viola Louise Hassenfeffer!" called her teacher. "Royalty does not dive."

"Sorry." Viola emptied her purse.

"And now," said Madame Gertrude, "Dance Lessons."

The princesses waltzed in circles,
in lines, and all around the room.

Princess Viola
was determined
to dazzle, but . . .

ZUP! ZOOM!

"Viola Louise Hassenfeffer!" called her teacher. "Royalty does not skateboard."

"Phooey." Viola let her boa fall to the floor.

Facts were facts.

Viola's day at Camp Princess was nearly over, and she was still a royal failure.

But then . . .

"HELP!" cried Madame Gertrude.
"A big green dragon!
SOMEONE CALL KNIGHT-1-1!"
Princesses ran here, there, and
everywhere in between.
But Viola Louise Hassenfeffer . . .

was not an ordinary princess.
She eyeballed that dragon and gave
it the best karate-chop she had.

HI-YAH!

SPL

The dragon stopped mid-puff.

Princess Viola climbed to
the top of the fountain and dove.

Princess Viola skateboarded in circles, in lines, and all around the room—

ZIP! ZUP! ZOOOM!

ASH!

The dragon sputtered.

until . . .

Princess Viola was a royal hero.
The other princesses crowded
around her.

"Well done!"

"Lovely!"

Princess Viola wasn't prim.

She wasn't proper. But . . .

she was the darling
of her kingdom anyway.

Chavela and the Magic Bubble

by **Monica Brown**

Illustrated by **Magaly Morales**

To my very own Chavela, who inspired this book with her
many magical questions —M.B.

To my sisters, Yuyi and Elizabeth, my pride
and inspiration —M.M.

Chevela loved to chew gum. She chewed pink bubblegum, rainbow-colored gum, sugar-free peppermint gum, and sour cherry gumballs. She liked gum that came in rolls, shredded gum, and teeny tiny gumballs that looked like confetti and felt slippery in her mouth. Chavela chomped her chicle every chance she got.

Chavela was especially good at blowing bubbles. She blew big bubbles shaped like pink balloons and little bubbles the size of jellybeans.

She could blow **bubbles** inside of **bubbles** and two **bubbles** side by side, and one time she even blew a bubble shaped like a dog.

On Saturdays, Chavela and her grandmother would split a piece of gum and go shopping on Market Street. Chavela's *abuelita* would tell her stories about the quiet town of Playa del Carmen, Mexico, where she grew up.

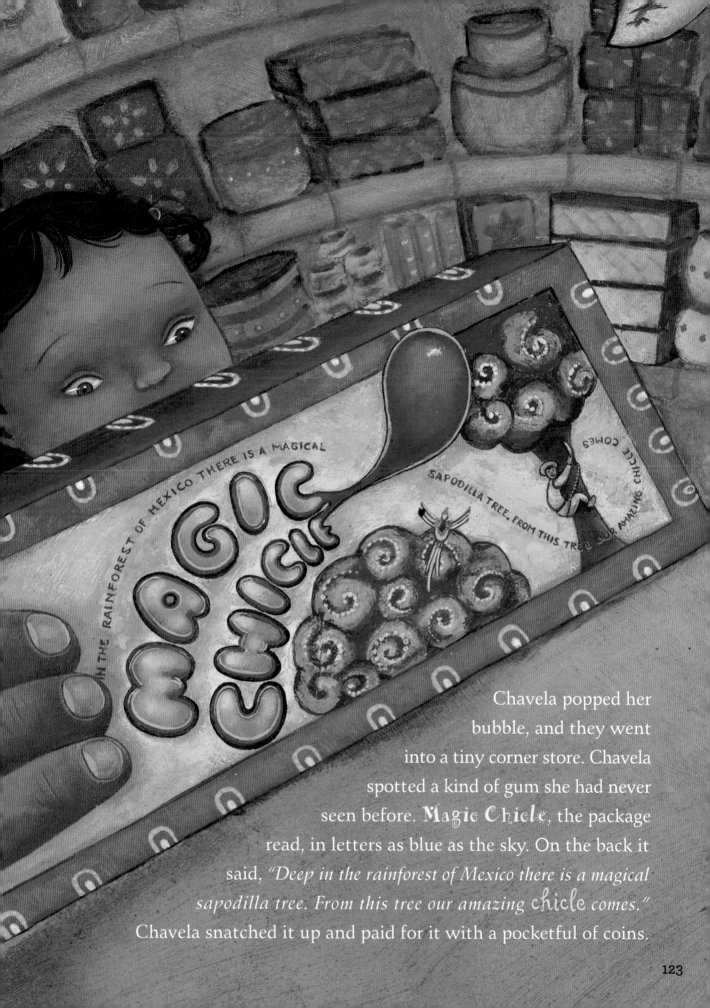

Chavela popped her bubble, and they went into a tiny corner store. Chavela spotted a kind of gum she had never seen before. Magic Chicle, the package read, in letters as blue as the sky. On the back it said, *"Deep in the rainforest of Mexico there is a magical sapodilla tree. From this tree our amazing chicle comes."* Chavela snatched it up and paid for it with a pocketful of coins.

On the way home, Chavela asked, "What does a tree have to do with gum?"

"Well, Chavela," explained Abuelita, "gum is made from chicle, the sap of the sapodilla tree. Did you know that my father was a chiclero? Chicleros are workers who care for the sapodilla trees and harvest chicle from them."

"But why is the chicle magic?"

"That you will have to find out for yourself," Abuelita said with a smile.

Once home, Chavela ran straight to her room and opened her Magic Chicle. It smelled wildly delicious. She popped a piece in her mouth . . . and then another . . . and another. Yum! Soon the whole package was gone.

Chavela chewed and chewed and then took a deep breath and blew a great big bubble that got bigger . . . and bigger . . . and bigger until . . .

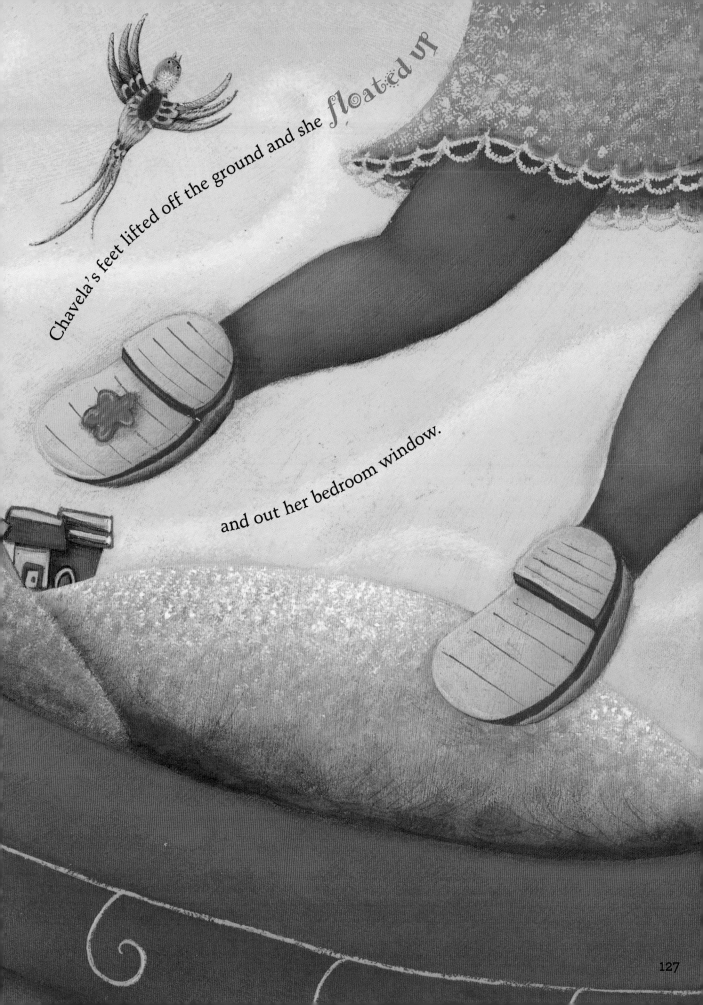

Chavela's feet lifted off the ground and she *floated up*

and out her bedroom window.

Then the wind blew Chavela and her magic **bubble** south toward Mexico and the white sand beaches of Playa del Carmen.

Chavela floated above the jungles of the Yucatán, bouncing along the tops of the lovely sapodilla trees.

Down below, *chicleros* were making zigzag cuts in the tree trunks and collecting the dripping chicle in big sacks. Children skipped around the trees, singing and holding hands. One little girl had a doll with a pretty **blue** dress. The girl waved and Chavela waved back.

Chavela floated softly down, landing under the tallest sapodilla
tree of all. The little girl with the doll came right up to Chavela
and said, "Hola! Do you like our magic tree?"

"Magic tree?" Chavela asked, her hand on the strong trunk.
"Why is it magic?"

"Because it brings us visitors like you!" the little girl said
with a wink.

Chavela held hands with the other children and together
they sang a song about the doll.

        Tengo una muñeca vestida de azul . . .

        I have a doll dressed up in blue . . .

Then they ran and played under the shade of the sapodilla
trees until Chavela became very tired. She wrapped herself up
in a pile of leaves and leaned against the magic tree. She watched
the butterflies and listened to the birds and the singing of the
chicleros, and soon she was fast asleep.

When Chavela woke up, the sun had set and the birds and the butterflies and the chicleros were gone. So were the little girl and the doll with the pretty blue dress. Chavela brushed the leaves away and shivered. She missed her abuelita. But she had already chewed all her magic gum. How would she ever get home?

Suddenly, she felt a drip on the tip of her nose. It was soft and sticky. It was chicle from the magic sapodilla tree!

Chavela popped the chicle into her mouth and chewed and chewed and blew and blew unitl . . . she floated UP and away into the twinkling sky, back over mountains and deserts and cities, finally drifting down,

down,

down,

toward her little   house.

Plop! Chavela floated through the window and landed on her bed, happy and bouncy and full of magic. She ran to the kitchen to see her grandmother. "Long journey?" Abuelita asked with a wink.

"How did you know?" Chavela asked.

"I know because when I was a little girl, magic was part of my life too. And now I have a special present I've been waiting to give you," Abuelita said. Then she reached deep into her pocket and pulled out the doll with the pretty blue dress. "This was mine when I was a little girl, and now it's yours, just like the magic of the sapodilla tree."

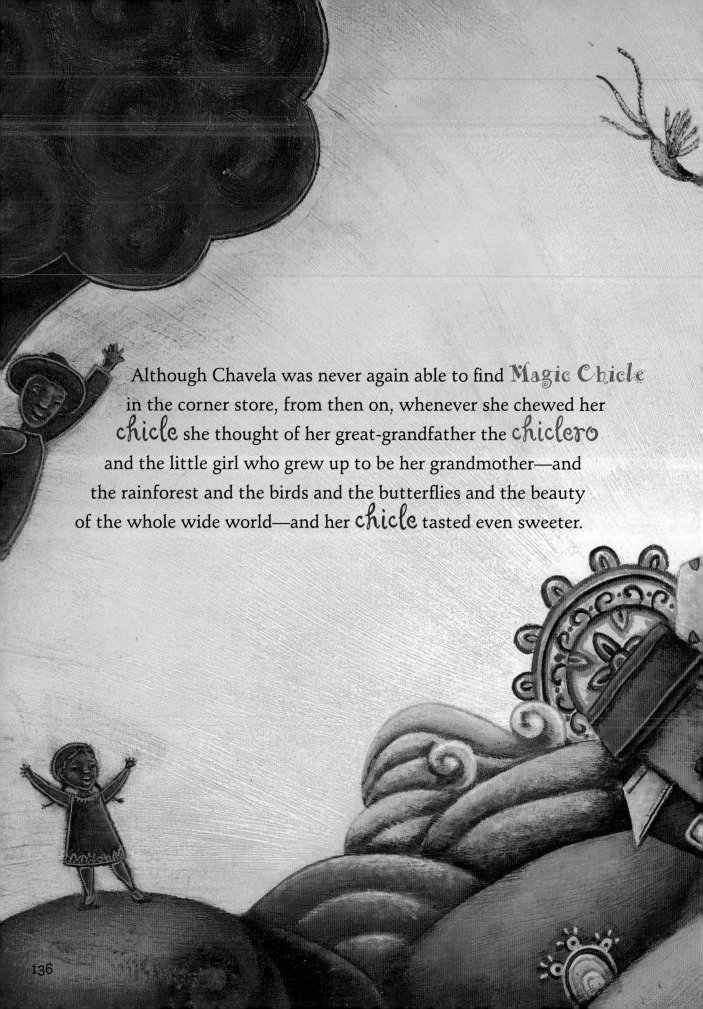

Although Chavela was never again able to find Magic Chicle in the corner store, from then on, whenever she chewed her chicle she thought of her great-grandfather the chiclero and the little girl who grew up to be her grandmother—and the rainforest and the birds and the butterflies and the beauty of the whole wide world—and her chicle tasted even sweeter.

Small Sister

Jessica Meserve

To my sister, Adria

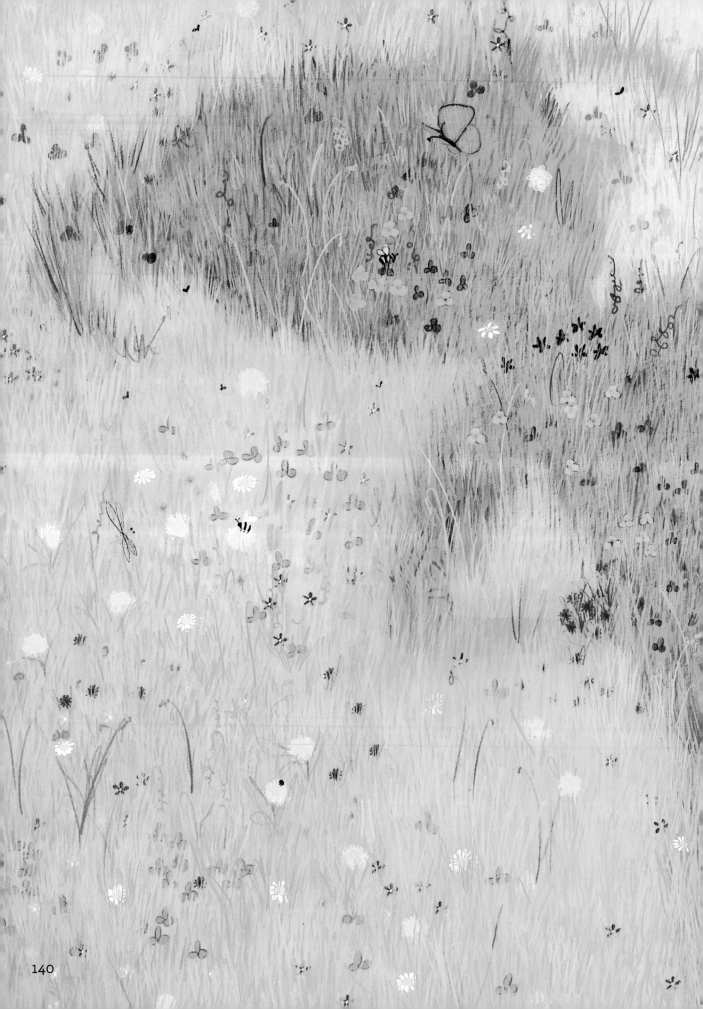

Small had a **problem.**
She was stuck in Big's shadow.

Small tried to jump higher,
but Big was bouncier.

Small tried to escape,
but Big was faster.

And Big always got
the best presents.

Sometimes Big tried
to scare Small.

One day Big made
Small very angry,

146

so Small did something
very mean.

Big's parrot
flew away.

But when Big
found out...

...Small felt
even smaller.

The next day,
Small decided
to leave.

Nobody noticed.

Small
was free.

She tried to feel happy,

but she
was too
lonely.

High in the tree,
Small saw Big's parrot.

Low on the ground,
Small saw...

...Big.
Big was too
scared to climb
the tree.

Small
wasn't
scared.

Small felt BRAVE.

Small felt BIG.

Small felt very happy.

And best of all,
Small was no longer
stuck in Big's shadow.

ELLA SARAH GETS DRESSED

Margaret Chodos-Irvine

For my own Ella Sarah
—M.C.I.

One morning, Ella Sarah got up and said,
"I want to wear my pink polka-dot pants,
my dress with orange-and-green flowers,
my purple-and-blue striped socks,
my yellow shoes,
and my red hat."

Her mother said,
"That outfit is too dressy.
Why don't you wear your nice
blue dress with matching socks,
and your white sandals?"

But Ella Sarah said, "No.
I want to wear my pink
polka-dot pants,
my dress with
orange-and-green
flowers, my
purple-and-blue
striped socks,
my yellow shoes,
and my red hat."

Her father said, "That outfit is too fancy.
Why don't you wear your yellow
T-shirt with white shorts, and
your tennis shoes?"

But Ella Sarah said, "No!
I want to wear my pink polka-dot pants,
my dress with orange-and-green flowers,
my purple-and-blue striped socks,
my yellow shoes,
and my red hat!"

Her big sister said, "That outfit is too silly. You should wear these overalls that are too small for me, and my old boots."

But Ella Sarah said, "NO!

I want to wear my pink polka-dot pants,

my dress with orange-and-green flowers,

my purple-and-blue striped socks,

my yellow shoes,

AND MY RED HAT!"

So...

she put on her pink polka-dot pants,

her dress with orange-and-green flowers,

**her purple-and-blue
striped socks**

her yellow shoes,

and her red hat.

Ella Sarah thought her outfit was just right.

DING DONG!

And so did her friends.

Cowgirl Kate and Cocoa

Written by **Erica Silverman**

Painted by **Betsy Lewin**

To Julia, the newest Torn —E.S   To horses everywhere —B.L.

Cowgirl Kate and her horse, Cocoa, were counting cows.

"Fifty-eight, fifty-nine—"

"There sure are a lot of cows," said Cocoa.

"Shhh!" said Cowgirl Kate.

"You are messing me up."

"I am hungry," said Cocoa.
"You are always hungry,"
said Cowgirl Kate.
Cocoa leaned down
and munched some grass.

Cowgirl Kate slid to the ground.

"I will count cows myself!" she said.

But she was too short.

She could not see all the cows.

She climbed up onto the fence,

but she still could not see all the cows.

She went to the tallest tree

and started to climb.

Up she went,

higher

and higher

and higher.

Cocoa galloped over.

"Come down, please!" he cried.

"I do not want you to fall."

"Don't worry," said Cowgirl Kate.

"I am a good climber."

"And *I* am a good worrier," said Cocoa.

"Please come down!

I will help you count cows."

Cowgirl Kate smiled.

She backed down the tree

and got into her saddle.

"Thank you," she said.

"Now I can see all the cows.

But I cannot remember

how many I counted."

"You counted fifty-nine," said Cocoa,

"and then I counted ten more."

Cowgirl Kate stared at him.

"But you were eating," she said.

"When did you do all that counting?"

Cocoa raised his head high.

"I am a talented cowhorse," he said.

"I can eat and count at the same time."

One night Cowgirl Kate slept in the barn.
"Good night, Cocoa," she said.
She crawled into her sleeping bag
and closed her eyes.

"Will you please fluff my straw?" Cocoa asked.

Cowgirl Kate sighed.

"I am very tired," she said.

But she climbed out of her sleeping bag and fluffed his straw. Then she crawled back into her sleeping bag.

"I am hungry,"
said Cocoa.
Cowgirl Kate sighed.
"You are always
hungry," she said.

But she climbed out of her sleeping bag
and gave him three carrots.
Then she crawled back into her sleeping bag.

"Uh-oh! My water bin is low," said Cocoa.

Cowgirl Kate groaned.

"Why didn't you tell me that before?"

"I didn't think of it before," said Cocoa.

"First I was thinking about straw.

Then I was thinking about food.

Now I am thinking about water."

"You are doing too much thinking,"
said Cowgirl Kate.

But she climbed out of her sleeping bag
and filled up his water bin.

"Is there anything else?" she asked.

"No," said Cocoa.

"Good," she said.

"Now think about sleep!"

"Good night, Katie," said Cocoa.

"Good night, Cocoa," said Cowgirl Kate.

The barn was cold.
Cowgirl Kate pulled the sleeping bag
up to her chin.
The moon was bright.
She pulled the sleeping bag
over her eyes.

An owl hooted outside.

Whoooooo. Whoooooo.

Cowgirl Kate shivered.

"Cocoa! I cannot sleep," she said.

"Then I will sing you a lullaby," said Cocoa.

"Rock-a-bye, cowgirl,
on your cowhorse.
Though the wind blows,
you'll never be tossed.
When the dawn breaks,
your cowhorse will say,
'My hat's on. I'm ready
to herd cows all day.'"

And Cowgirl Kate smiled,
snuggled close . . .
and fell asleep.

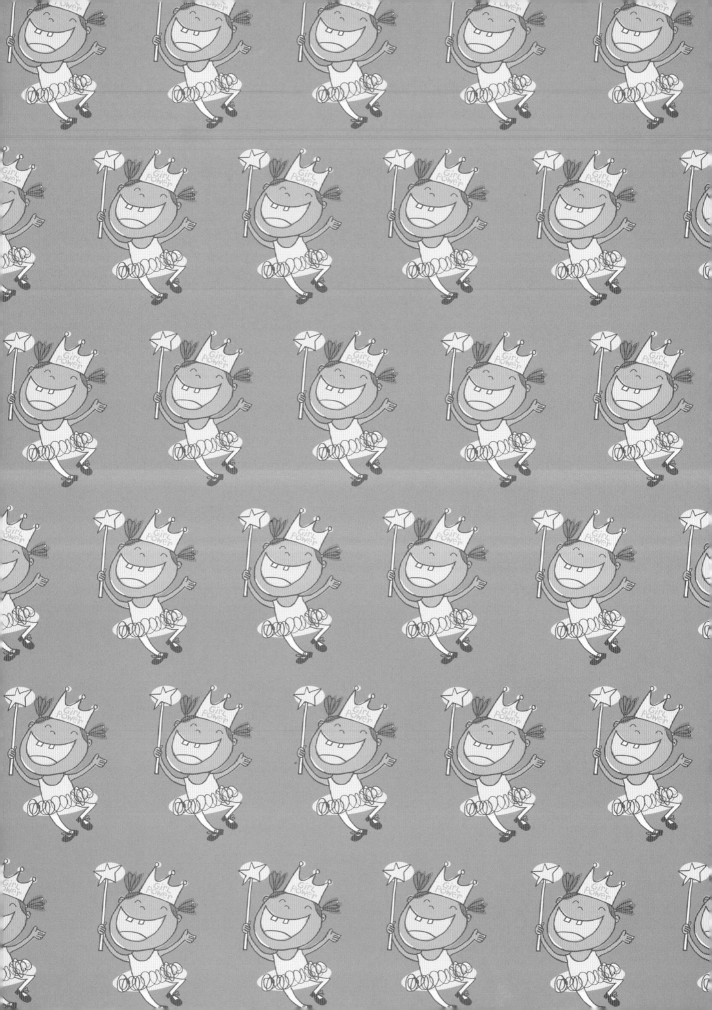

WOW!
It Sure Is Good to Be You!

Written and Illustrated by Cynthia Jabar

Somebody, somewhere,
is thinking about you,

Keeps your picture in their pocket,

Misses your kisses,

Loves you more than birds love trees,
more than brothers love to tease,
loves you even more than dogs have fleas,
and that's a lot, too!

Loving you is their favorite thing to do.

WOW!

It sure is good to be you!

Somebody, somewhere,
remembers your silly faces,
and sad ones, too,
wishes you all the luck
in the universe,

Is always very proud of you!

Somebody, somewhere, is missing you, too,

Loves you no matter what you say or do,

Loves you
toe-tap-happy
loud,

Or sad, quiet blue,
loves you more than cows moo moo,
more than ballerinas wear tutus,
would even ride a smelly yak from Kathmandu,
just to be with you!
And that's really far, too!

WOW!

It sure is good to be you!

Somebody, somewhere
knows you're cool-girl
brave and strong,

With amazing talents.
Why, even your short list
goes on and on and on . . .

And now,
somebody, somewhere,
is coming to visit,
to love you and laugh,
and share some special time.

216

Because now is the gift,
and now you're all mine!

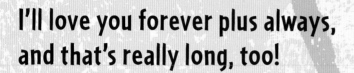

I'll love you forever plus always,
and that's really long, too!

218

WOW!

It sure is good to be you!

ABOUT THE AUTHORS AND ILLUSTRATORS

KAREN BEAUMONT is the *New York Times* best-selling author of many books for children, including *I Ain't Gonna Paint No More!*, *Move Over, Rover!*, *No Sleep for the Sheep!*, and *Shoe-La-La!*. Karen hopes *I Like Myself!* encourages children to see themselves as God sees them: with unconditional love. For amidst that quality of love and self-acceptance, the best in them will thrive. Visit her at www.karenbeaumont.com.

DAVID CATROW is an editorial cartoonist and the illustrator of more than seventy books for children, including the *New York Times* bestseller *Ain't Gonna Paint No More!* by Karen Beaumont and his own Max Spaniel series. He lives in Ohio with his wife and their three dogs. His website is www.catrow.com.

BETH CADENA lives on the southern coast of Maine with one super husband, two super daughters, a super cat, and a super dog. *Supersister* is her first book.

FRANK W. DORMER is the author/illustrator of *Socksquatch* and *The Obstinate Pen,* and the illustrator of the acclaimed Aggie and Ben series and the superhero series The Adventures of Jo Schmo. Frank is an elementary school art teacher who lives with his family in Connecticut. Visit his website at www.frankwdormer.com.

MARILYN SINGER is the author of more than one hundred books for children. She lives in Brooklyn, New York, and Washington, Connecticut. For more information, please visit www.marilynsinger.net.

ALEXANDRA BOIGER has illustrated several picture and chapter books, among them *Poor Doreen: A Fishy Tale, Tallulah's Tutu* and its sequels, and the chapter book series The Magical Animal Adoption Agency. Originally from Munich, Germany, she now lives in California. Please visit her at www.alexandraboiger.com.

JEANNE BIRDSALL is the National Book Award–winning author of *The Penderwicks* and its sequels, *The Penderwicks on Gardam Street* and *The Penderwicks at Point Mouette,* all of which were *New York Times* bestsellers. She lives in Northampton, Massachusetts, with her husband, three insane cats, and a stubborn Boston terrier named Cagney. Visit her website at www.jeannebirdsall.com.

MATT PHELAN's many books include *Very Hairy Bear* by Alice Schertle and *The Storm in the Barn,* winner of the Scott O'Dell Award. He lives in Philadelphia. Visit www.mattphelan.com.

TAMMI SAUER, a former teacher and library media specialist, is the author of *Princess in Training, Nugget and Fang,* and many other picture books. She lives in Edmond, Oklahoma. Visit her website at www.tammisauer.com.

JOE BERGER is an author and illustrator of many popular picture books, as well as an animator and cartoonist. He lives in Bristol, England, with his family. Visit his website at www.joeberger.co.uk.

MONICA BROWN is the author of several award-winning bilingual books inspired by her Peruvian American heritage and is a frequent conference speaker. She lives in Flagstaff, Arizona, and is an associate professor of English at NAU, specializing in U.S. Latino and multicultural literature. You can learn more about her at www.monicabrown.net.

MAGALY MORALES is the illustrator of *A Piñata in a Pine Tree* by Pat Mora and *What Can You Do with a Paleta?* by Carmen Tafolla. She lives in Mexico. Visit her at www.magalymorales.com.

JESSICA MESERVE was born in Maine, spent much of her childhood in New Hampshire, and now lives in the U.K. with her two children. She studied illustration at Edinburgh College of Art and worked in publishing as a children's book designer before going freelance to pursue a career as an illustrator. *Small Sister* is the first book she has both written and illustrated.

MARGARET CHODOS-IRVINE's vivid, innovative art has appeared on many book jackets and in several children's books. She was recognized with a Caldecott Honor Award for *Ella Sarah Gets Dressed.* She lives in Seattle, Washington. Visit Margaret at www.chodos-irvine.com.

ERICA SILVERMAN received a Theodor Seuss Geisel Honor for *Cowgirl Kate and Cocoa,* the first of six books about the pair. In addition, she has written many books for children, including *Hanukkah Hop, Big Pumpkin,* and *Don't Fidget a Feather.* She lives in Los Angeles, California. Visit www.ericasilverman.com.

BETSY LEWIN is the well-known illustrator of *Duck for President; Giggle, Giggle, Quack;* and the Caldecott Honor–winning *Click, Clack, Moo: Cows That Type,* all written by Doreen Cronin. She lives in New York City.

CYNTHIA JABAR is the illustrator of a number of books for children, including *Rain Song* and *Snow Dance.* Her distinctive illustrations have been described by reviewers as "vigorous," "full of zest," and "bright and saucy." She divides her time between Portland, Maine, and New York City. You can visit her at cynthiajabarkids.com.